W9-CRM-505

The Secret Society of Monster Hunters

The Werewolf's Curse

by Kate Tremaine
illustrated by Jared Sams

TORCH GRAPHIC PRESS

Published in the United States of America by Cherry Lake Publishing Group
Ann Arbor, Michigan
www.cherrylakepublishing.com

Reading Adviser: Marla Conn, MS, Ed., Literacy specialist, Read-Ability, Inc.

Book Design: Book Buddy Media

Photo Credits: page 1: ©svekloid / Shutterstock; page 5: ©CSA-Images/Vetta / Getty Images; page 11: ©Thomas J. Halloran / Wikimedia; page 21: ©Nastasic/DigitalVision Vectors / Getty Images; page 27: ©Tatiana Kasyanova / Shutterstock; page 27: ©cepera / Shutterstock; page 27: ©UyUy / Shutterstock; page 30: ©Richard Lewisohn/DigitalVision / Getty Images; background: ©OpenClipart-Vectors / Pixabay (facts); background: ©MarjanNo / Pixabay (lined paper); background: ©Chiken_brave / Shutterstock; background: ©Lukiyanova Natalia frenta / Shutterstock (sidebars)

Torch Graphic Press is an imprint of Cherry Lake Publishing Group.

Library of Congress Cataloging-in-Publication Data has been filed and is available at catalog.loc.gov

Cherry Lake Publishing Group would like to acknowledge the work of the Partnership for 21st Century Learning, a Network of Battelle for Kids. Please visit http://www.battelleforkids.org/networks/p21 for more information.

Printed in the United States of America
Corporate Graphics

TABLE OF CONTENTS

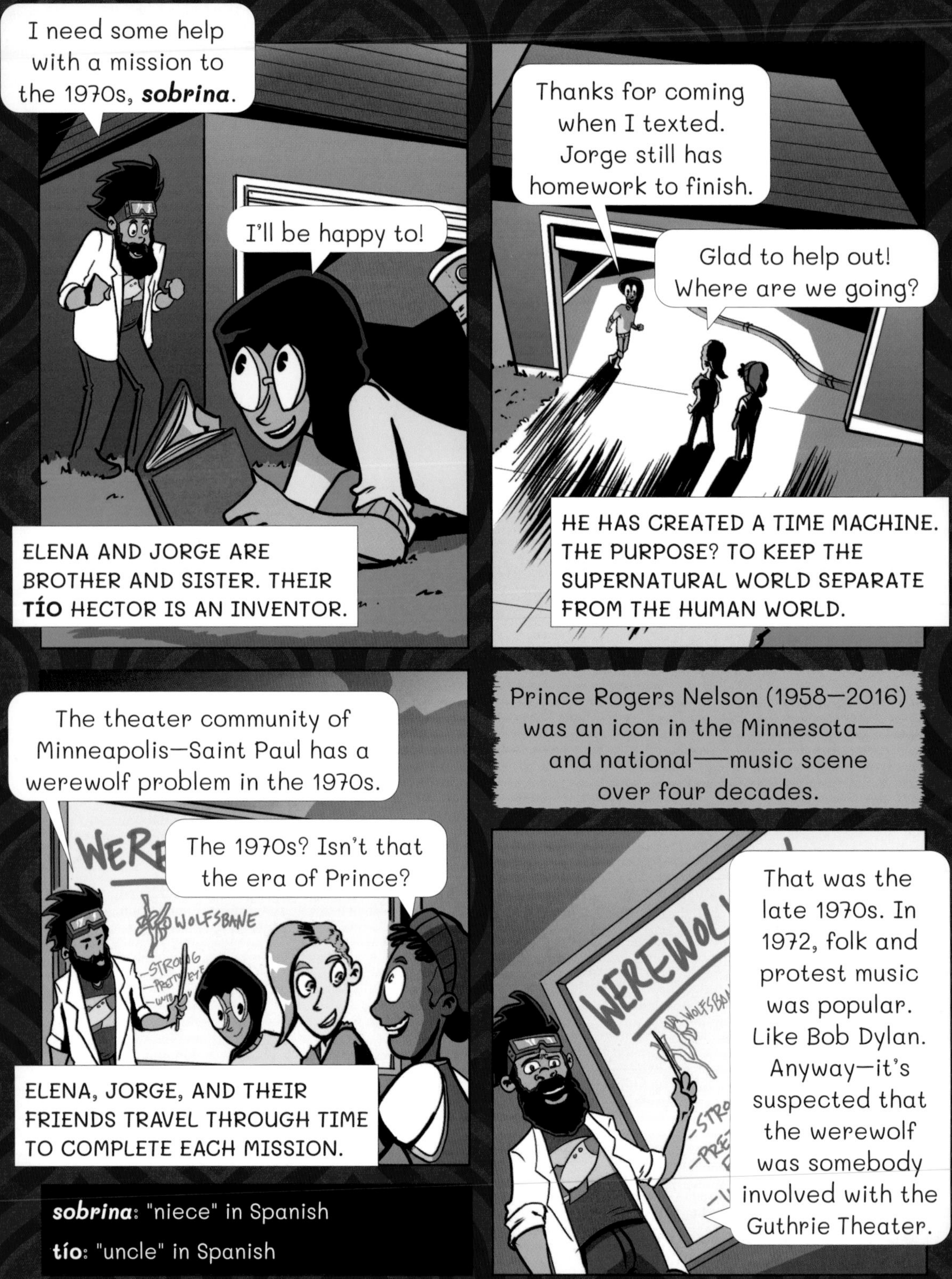
I need some help with a mission to the 1970s, ***sobrina***.
I'll be happy to!
ELENA AND JORGE ARE BROTHER AND SISTER. THEIR **TÍO** HECTOR IS AN INVENTOR.
Thanks for coming when I texted. Jorge still has homework to finish.
Glad to help out! Where are we going?
HE HAS CREATED A TIME MACHINE. THE PURPOSE? TO KEEP THE SUPERNATURAL WORLD SEPARATE FROM THE HUMAN WORLD.
The theater community of Minneapolis–Saint Paul has a werewolf problem in the 1970s.
The 1970s? Isn't that the era of Prince?
WOLFSBANE
ELENA, JORGE, AND THEIR FRIENDS TRAVEL THROUGH TIME TO COMPLETE EACH MISSION.
Prince Rogers Nelson (1958–2016) was an icon in the Minnesota—and national—music scene over four decades.
WEREWOL
That was the late 1970s. In 1972, folk and protest music was popular. Like Bob Dylan. Anyway—it's suspected that the werewolf was somebody involved with the Guthrie Theater.

sobrina: "niece" in Spanish

tío: "uncle" in Spanish

WHAT IS A WEREWOLF?

A werewolf is a human who changes into a dangerous wolf creature. This change is not in the person's control. It happens during a full moon. If you are bitten by a werewolf, you become a werewolf. What else is known about these creatures?

* Werewolves look like large wolves.

* They are extremely strong and fast.

* Their **transformations** happen only at night. This change can be confusing to new werewolves. Older werewolves are less dangerous.

* They do not attack people unless they are afraid.

* In human form, werewolves are hard to spot. But they may be tired around the full moon, because they hunt all night.

* They may have eyebrows that meet in the middle.

* They will probably have very beautiful and noticeable eyes.

transformations: changes in form or appearance

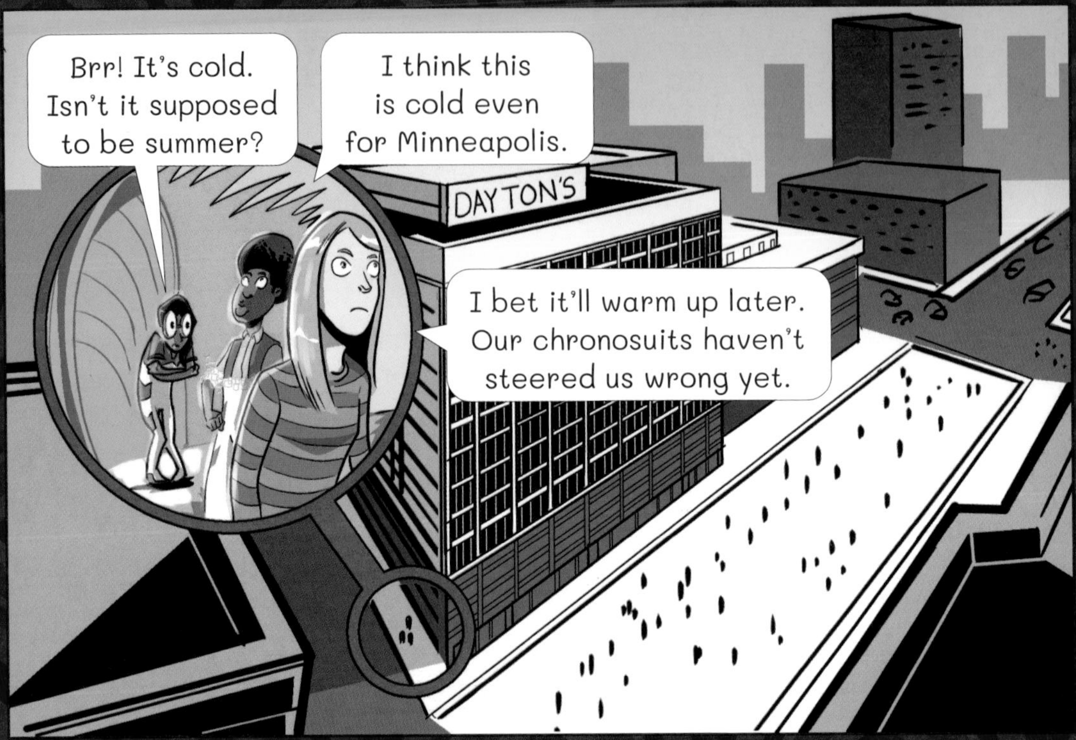
Brr! It's cold. Isn't it supposed to be summer?
I think this is cold even for Minneapolis.
DAYTON'S
I bet it'll warm up later. Our chronosuits haven't steered us wrong yet.

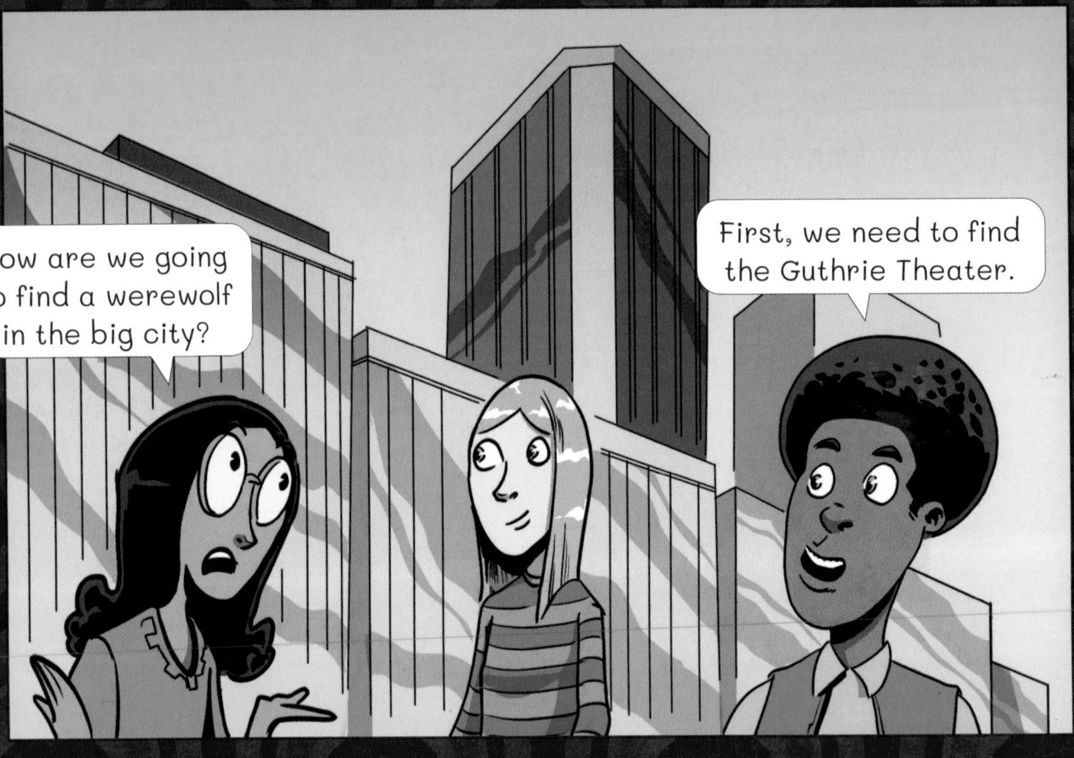
How are we going to find a werewolf in the big city?
First, we need to find the Guthrie Theater.

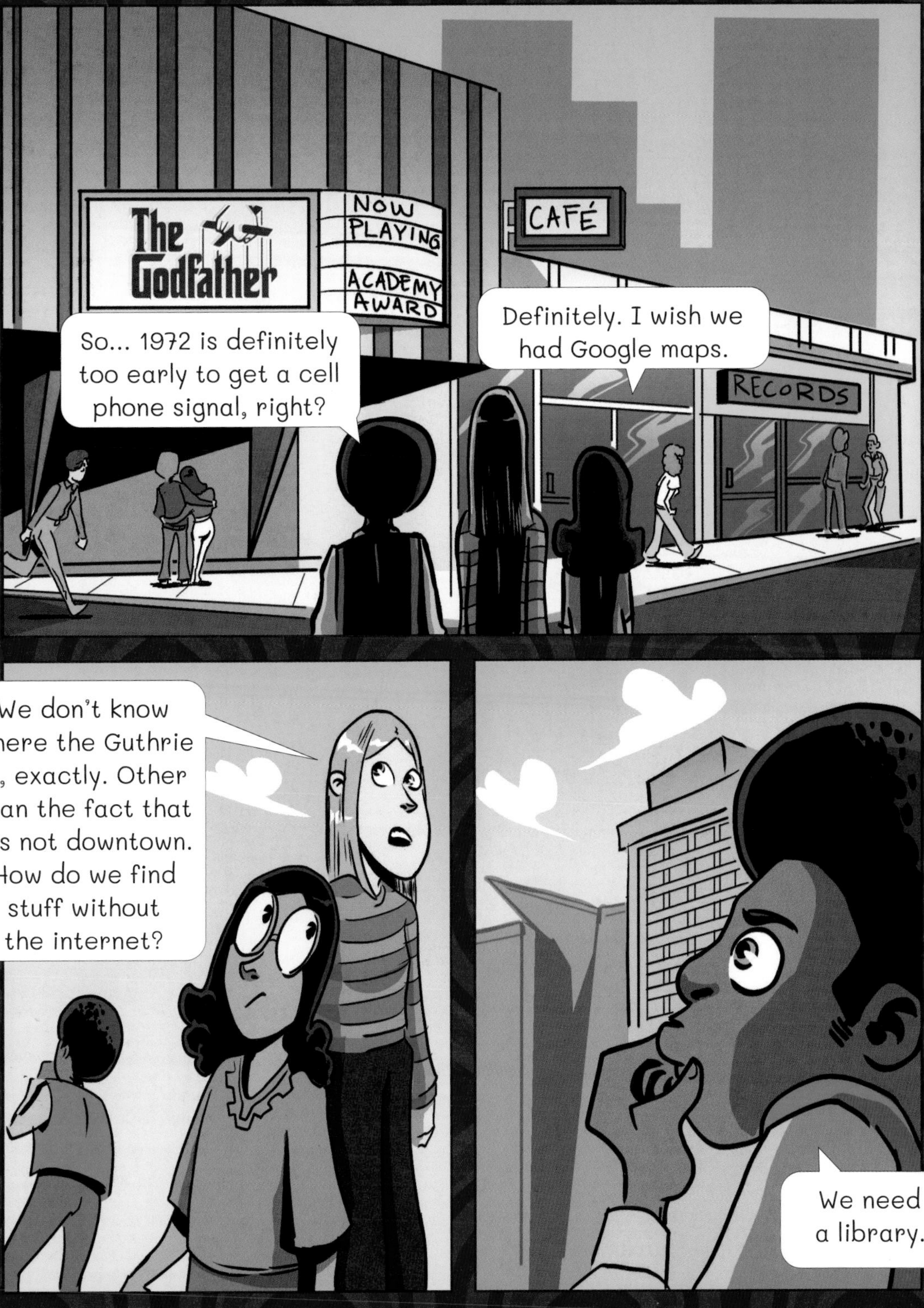
The Godfather
NOW PLAYING
ACADEMY AWARD
CAFÉ
RECORDS
So... 1972 is definitely too early to get a cell phone signal, right?
Definitely. I wish we had Google maps.
We don't know where the Guthrie is, exactly. Other than the fact that it's not downtown. How do we find stuff without the internet?
We need a library.

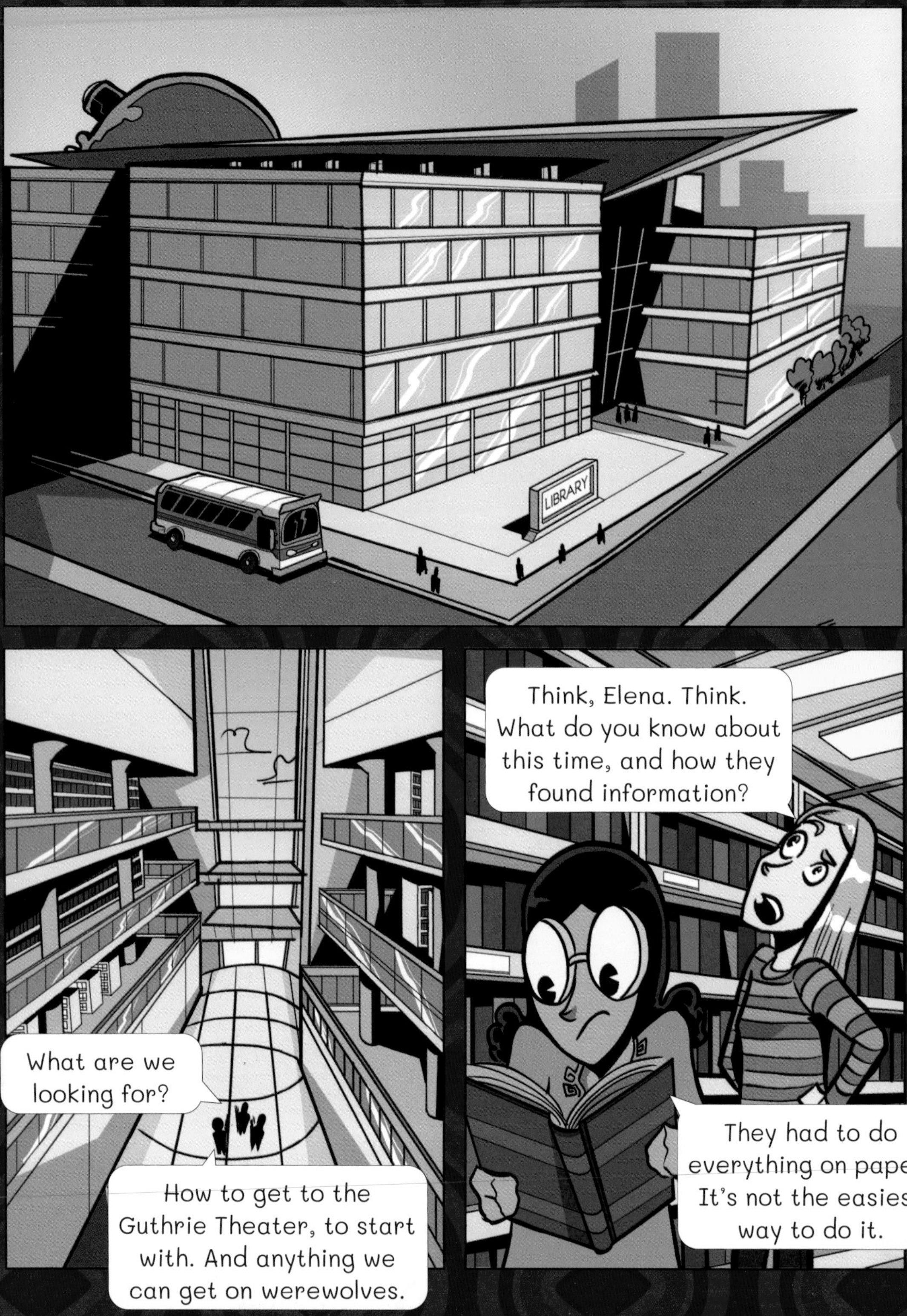

LIBRARY
What are we looking for?
How to get to the Guthrie Theater, to start with. And anything we can get on werewolves.
Think, Elena. Think. What do you know about this time, and how they found information?
They had to do everything on paper. It's not the easiest way to do it.

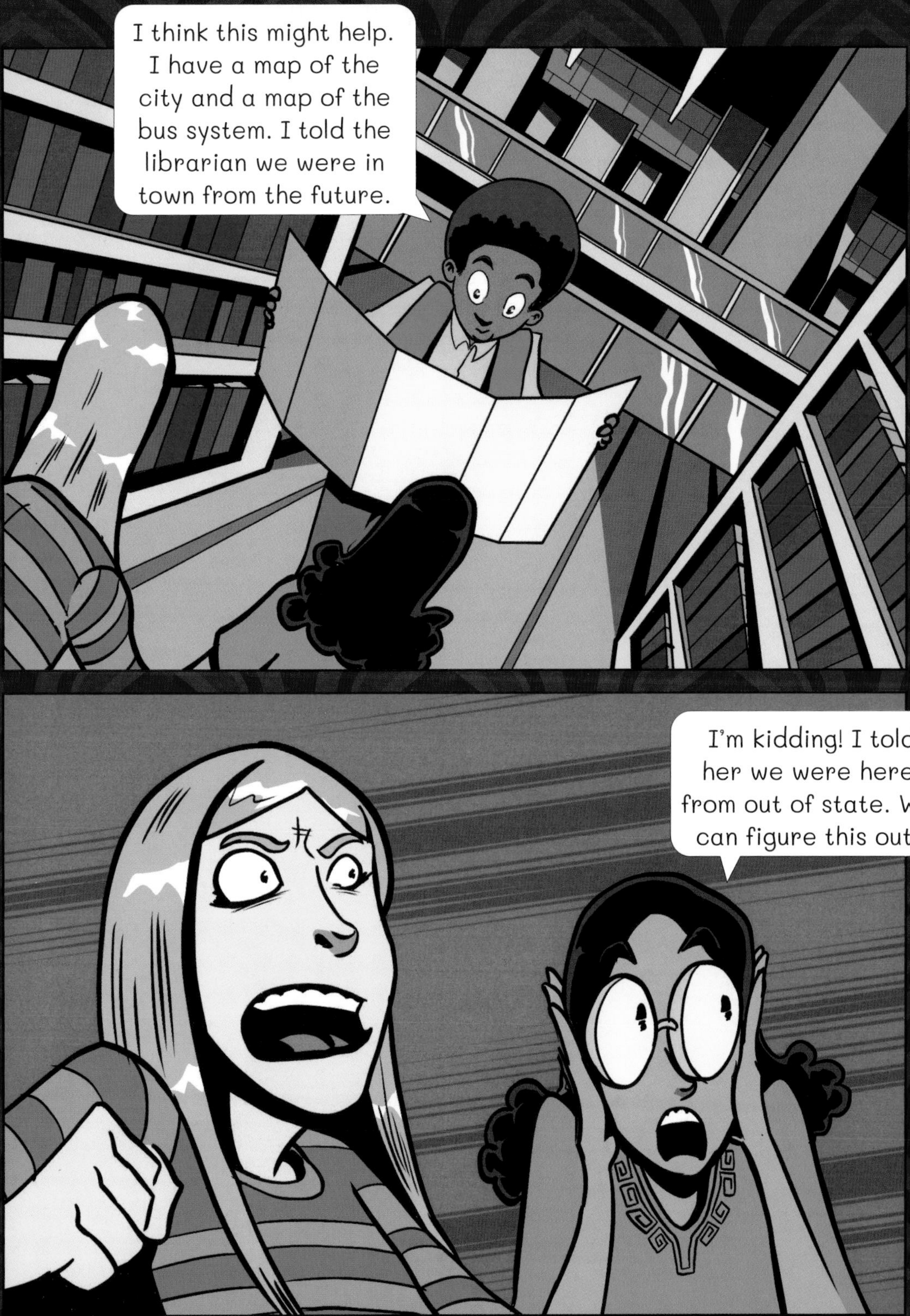
I think this might help. I have a map of the city and a map of the bus system. I told the librarian we were in town from the future.
I'm kidding! I told her we were here from out of state. We can figure this out.

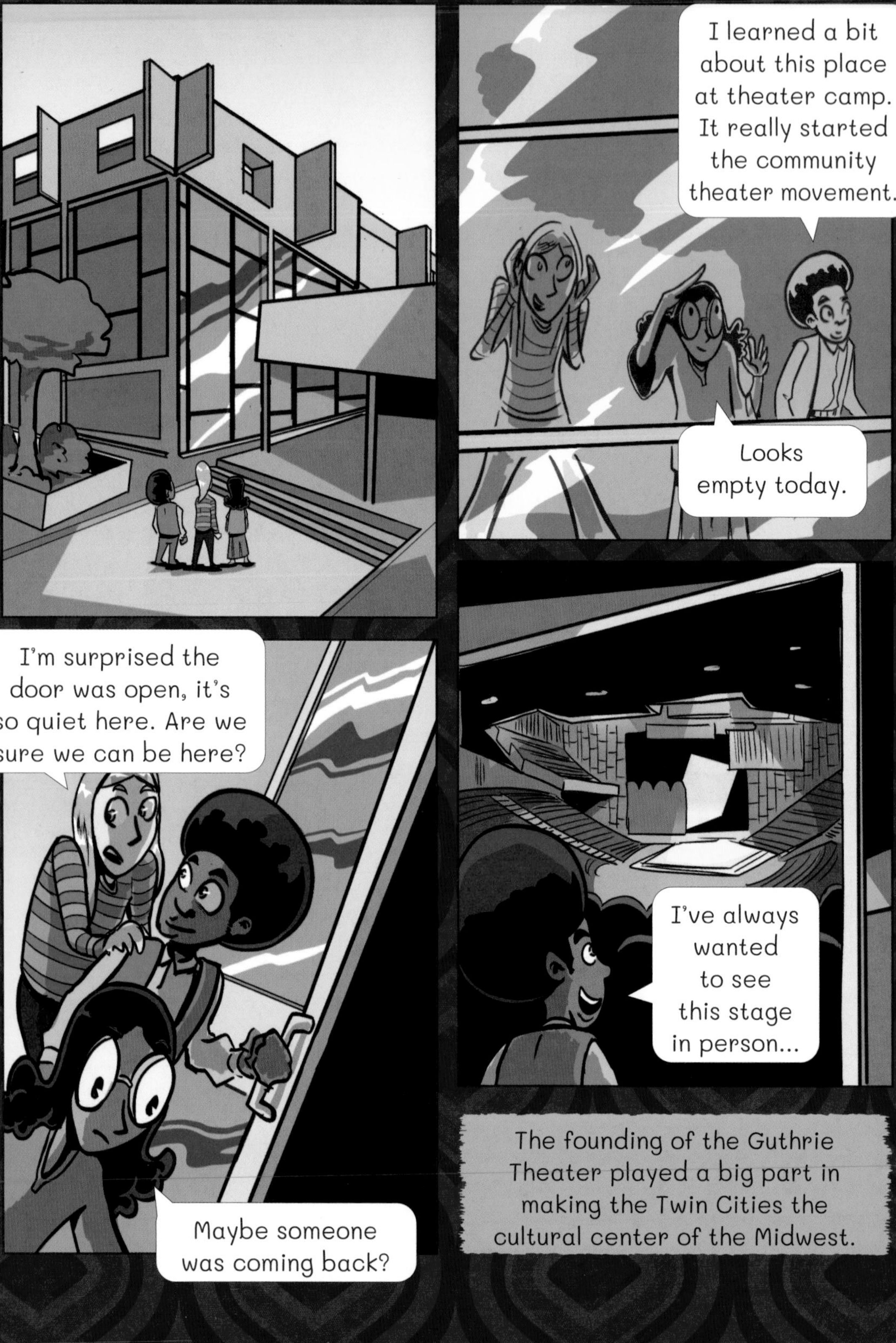
I learned a bit about this place at theater camp. It really started the community theater movement.
Looks empty today.
I'm surprised the door was open, it's so quiet here. Are we sure we can be here?
Maybe someone was coming back?
I've always wanted to see this stage in person...
The founding of the Guthrie Theater played a big part in making the Twin Cities the cultural center of the Midwest.

TIPS FOR THE DECADE

* The early 1970s were similar to the 1960s. The Vietnam War was still a defining event. The **draft** continued until late 1972. The war made many Americans lose faith in the government.
* Many people were still fighting for equal rights. This included African Americans, women, Native Americans, and **Chicanos**.

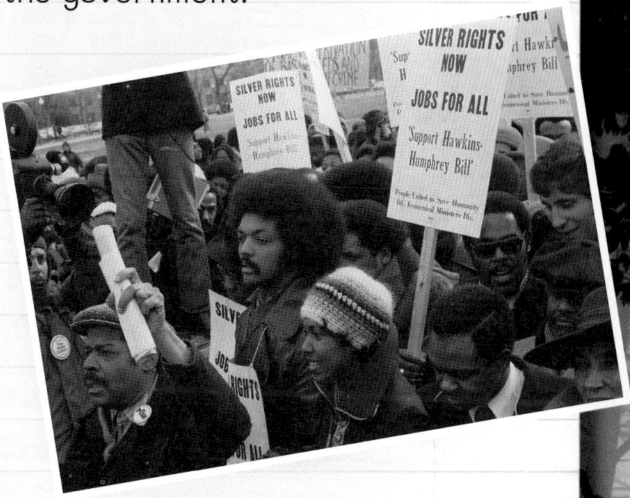
SILVER RIGHTS NOW
JOBS FOR ALL
'Support Hawkins-Humphrey Bill'

* Awareness of environmental issues also started growing in the 1970s.
* The 1970s was sometimes called the "Me Decade."
* Folk music, rock 'n' roll, heavy metal, funk, and disco were popular forms of music.
* On television, women became main characters for the first time. Women were becoming more important in many jobs across the country, too.

draft: when the government forces people to join the military

Chicanos: people of Mexican descent who live in the United States

Hey, you must have forgotten. The **repertory** program's at the Fair today—it's Fair Day.
ROMEO + JULIET
MLET
Fair Day?
Everyone's at the State Fair for opening-day promotions and stuff... You must be from out of town. Everyone knows Fair Day.
What's the easiest way to get there?
The bus'll get you there. Look for the State Fair Express route, can't miss it.

repertory: regular performances by a theater company

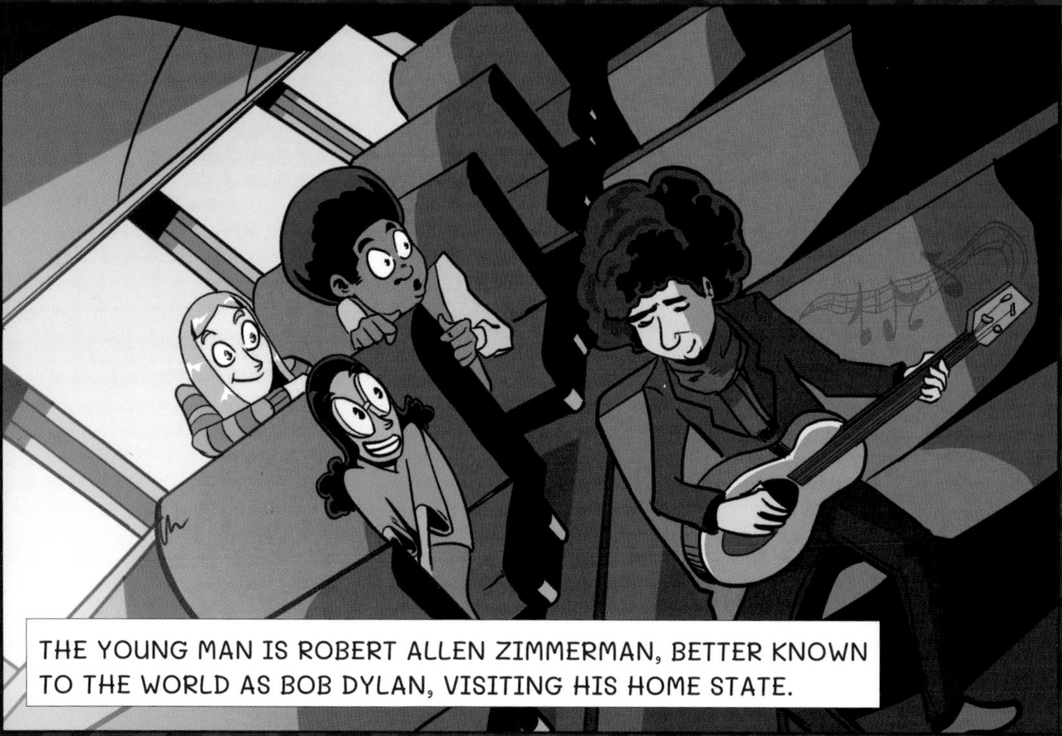
THE YOUNG MAN IS ROBERT ALLEN ZIMMERMAN, BETTER KNOWN TO THE WORLD AS BOB DYLAN, VISITING HIS HOME STATE.

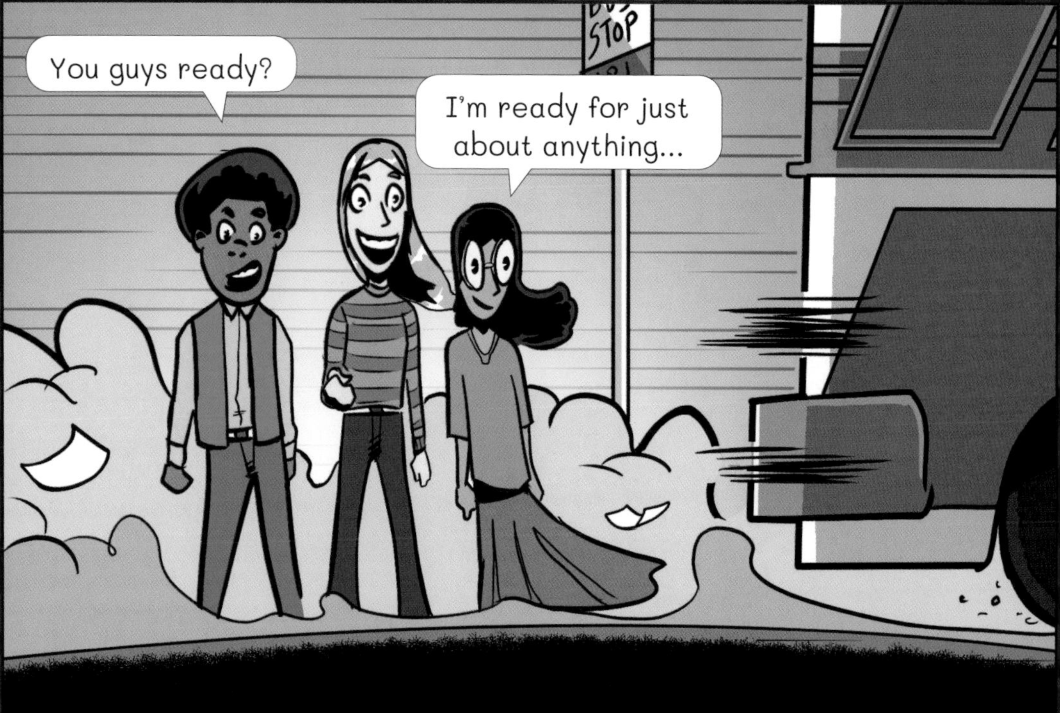
STOP
You guys ready?
I'm ready for just about anything...

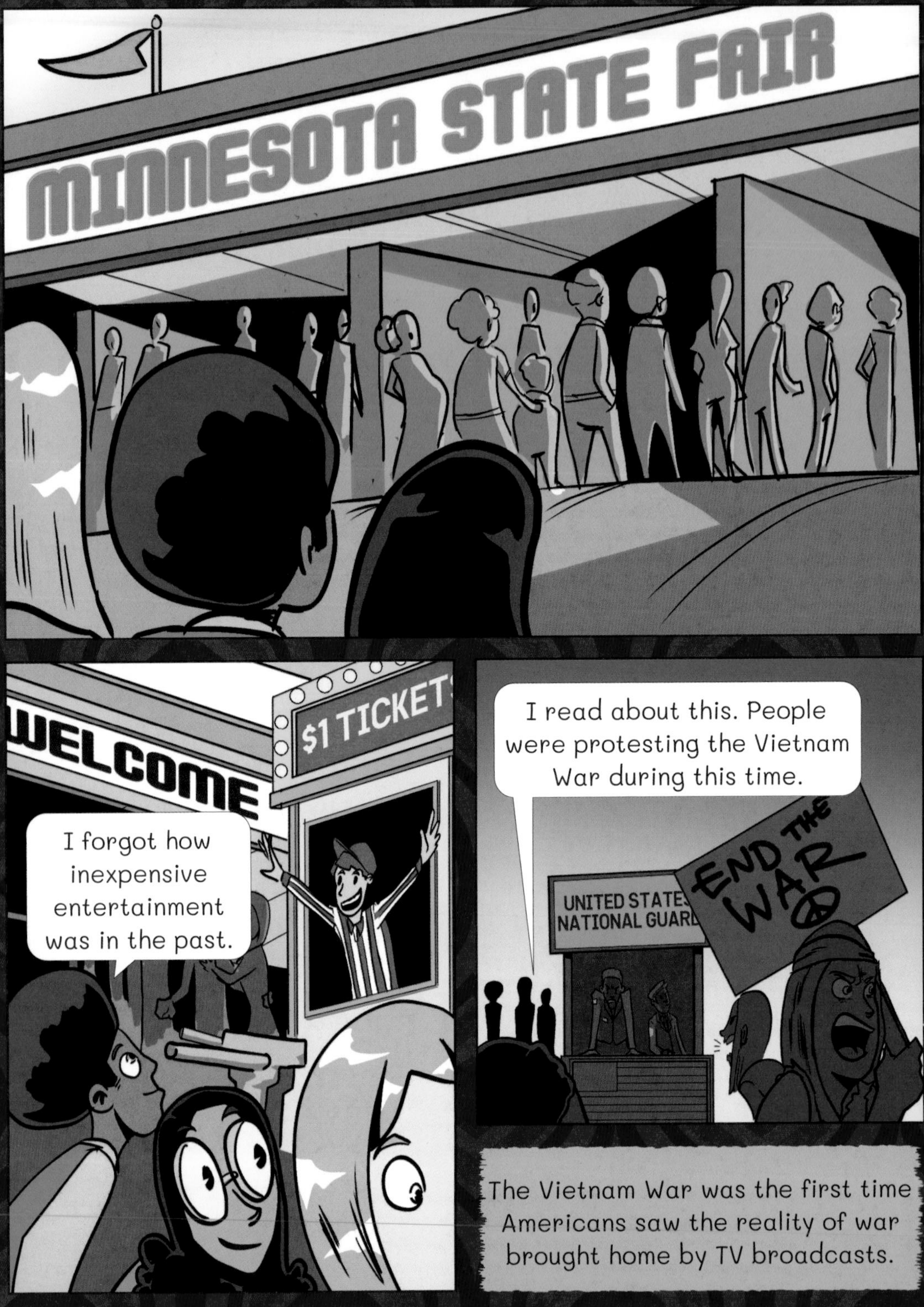
MINNESOTA STATE FAIR
WELCOME
$1 TICKETS
I forgot how inexpensive entertainment was in the past.
I read about this. People were protesting the Vietnam War during this time.
UNITED STATES NATIONAL GUARD
END THE WAR
The Vietnam War was the first time Americans saw the reality of war brought home by TV broadcasts.

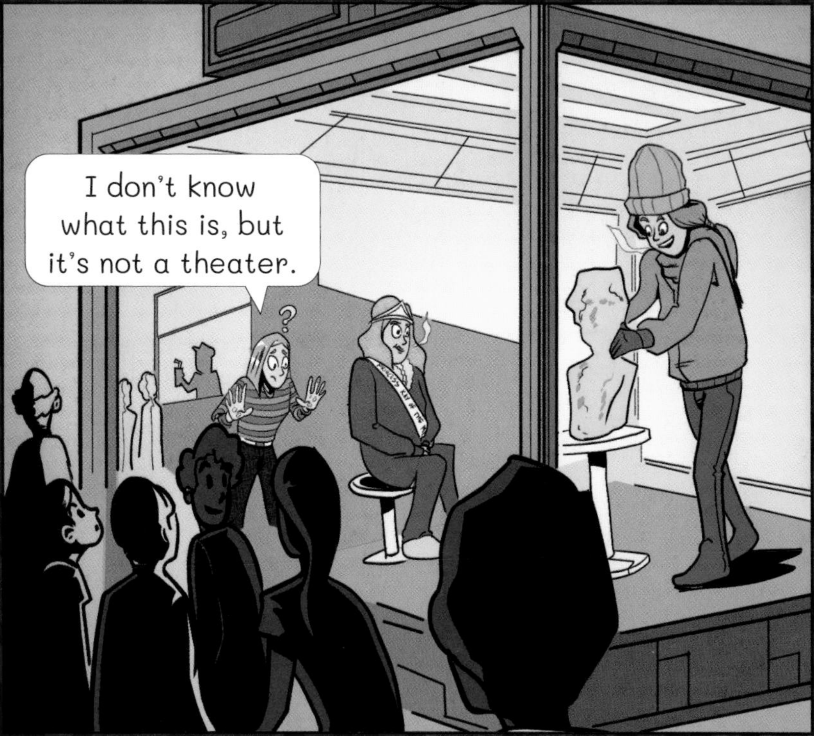
I don't know what this is, but it's not a theater.

The butter carving of small-town dairy princess, Princess Kay of the Milky Way, is a famous event at the Minnesota State Fair. The primary carver, Linda Christiansen, started at the Fair in 1972.

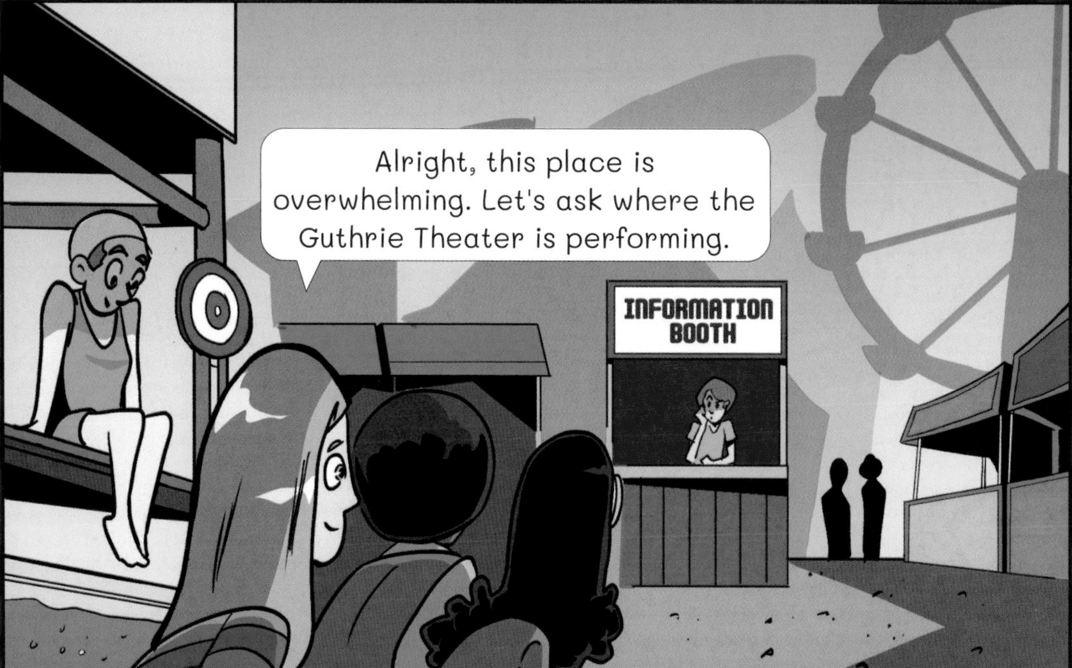
Alright, this place is overwhelming. Let's ask where the Guthrie Theater is performing.
INFORMATION BOOTH

Here we are!

Today: Guthrie Theater Presentation

Kent banish'd thus! And France in choler parted! And the king gone to-night! Subscribed his power!

I did *A Midsummer Night's Dream* in middle school. I know these lines.

Oh, that's my favorite. It's so much fun for **production**, with all the magic.

YAAAAWN

Guthrie Summer Repertory Program

production: in theater, a group in charge of the practical aspects of a play, like set design and lights; the process involved in making a play

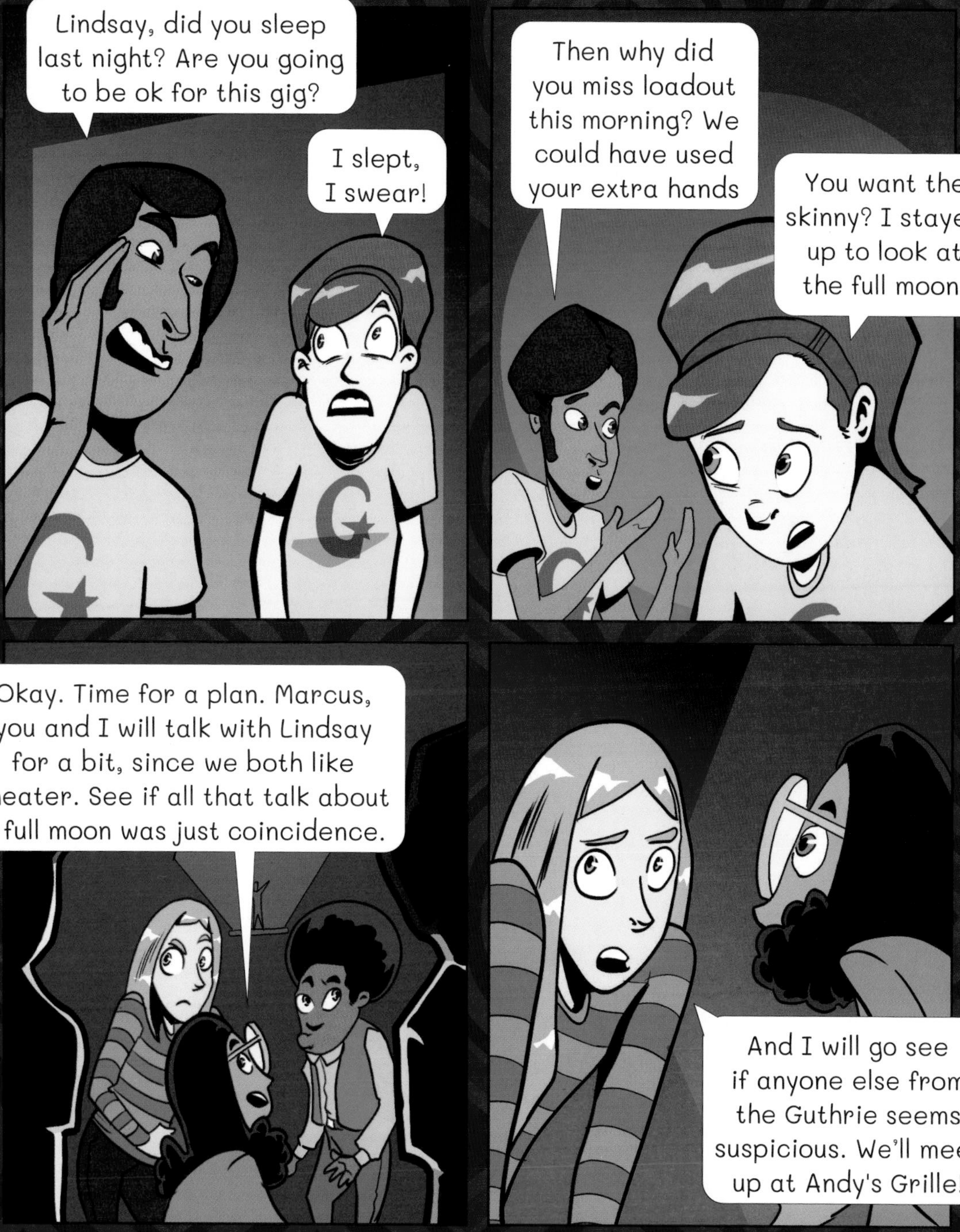
Lindsay, did you sleep last night? Are you going to be ok for this gig?
I slept, I swear!
Then why did you miss loadout this morning? We could have used your extra hands
You want the skinny? I stayed up to look at the full moon.
Okay. Time for a plan. Marcus, you and I will talk with Lindsay for a bit, since we both like theater. See if all that talk about a full moon was just coincidence.
And I will go see if anyone else from the Guthrie seems suspicious. We'll meet up at Andy's Grille!

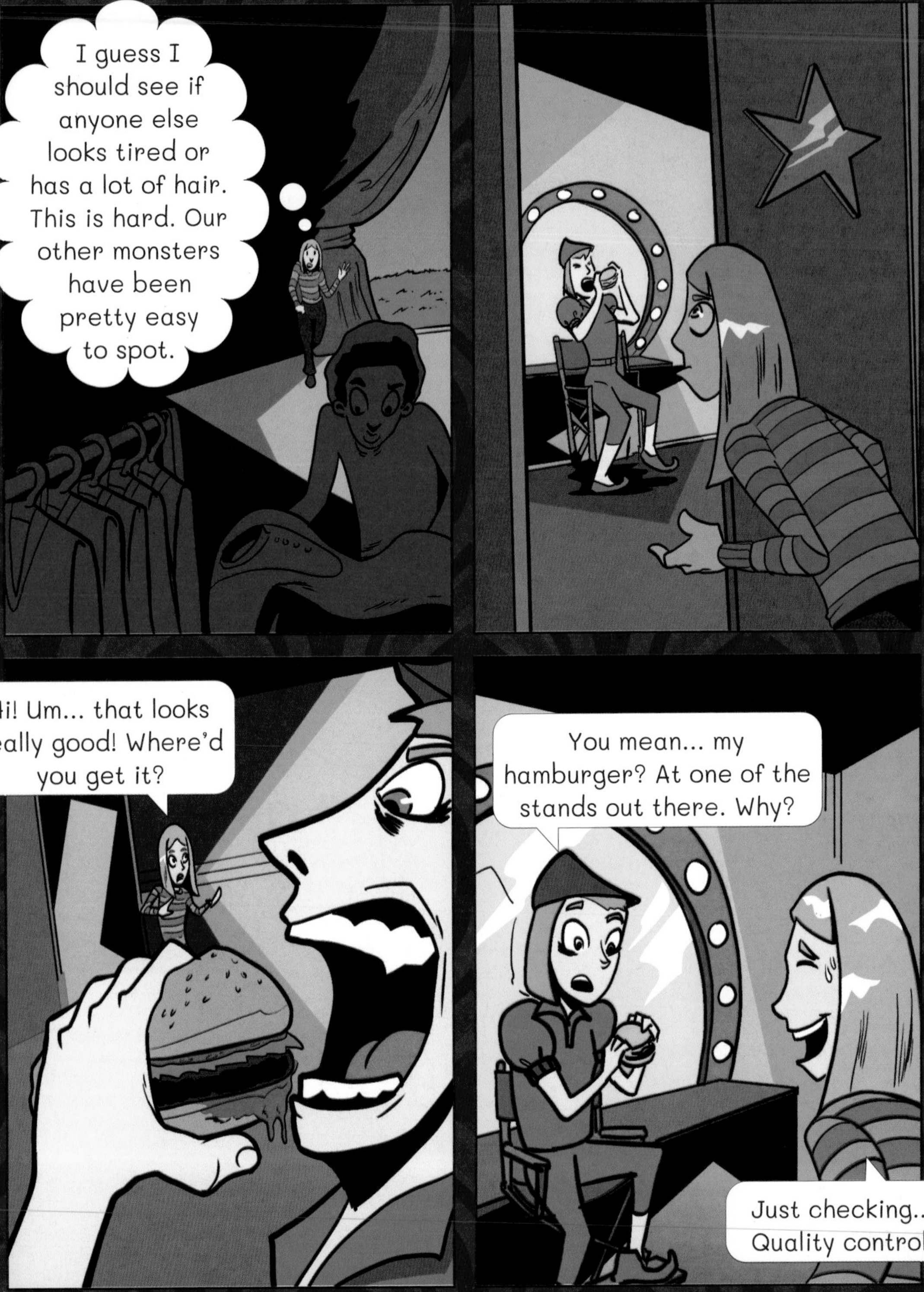
I guess I should see if anyone else looks tired or has a lot of hair. This is hard. Our other monsters have been pretty easy to spot.
Hi! Um... that looks really good! Where'd you get it?
You mean... my hamburger? At one of the stands out there. Why?
Just checking... Quality control!

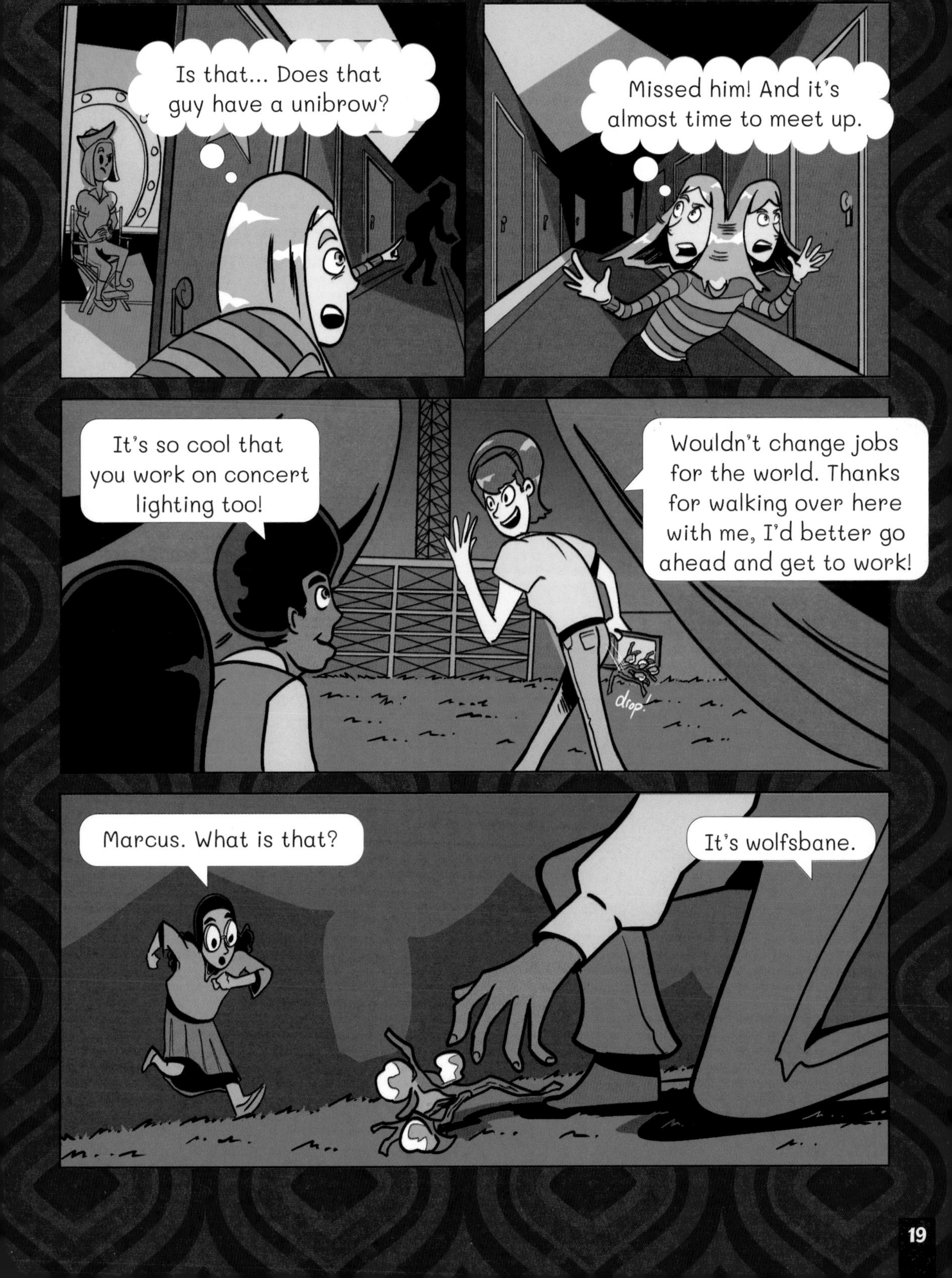
Is that... Does that guy have a unibrow?
Missed him! And it's almost time to meet up.
It's so cool that you work on concert lighting too!
Wouldn't change jobs for the world. Thanks for walking over here with me, I'd better go ahead and get to work!
drop!
Marcus. What is that?
It's wolfsbane.

I didn't find a thing. Did you guys?

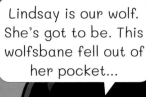

Lindsay is our wolf. She's got to be. This wolfsbane fell out of her pocket...

It's pretty. And pretty poisonous.

I hope you know what you're doing.

I don't, but winging it has worked so far. Let's go find her.

WEREWOLF SURVIVAL TIPS

How can you survive an encounter with such a dangerous creature? Werewolves have a number of weaknesses.

* Werewolves hate silver. Silver is pure. It's connected to the moon. It won't kill werewolves. But it will weaken them.
* Werewolves hate the wolfsbane plant. It has poison. It may keep werewolves human.
* Werewolves also hate salt. Salt sucks water from their bodies.
* To stop from being attacked, cover up your human smell. Rub mud on your clothes and skin.
* Stay in crowds, especially at night. Werewolves stay away from crowds.
* Don't be aggressive. This'll make werewolves mad. Werewolves are half-human. They understand your words.

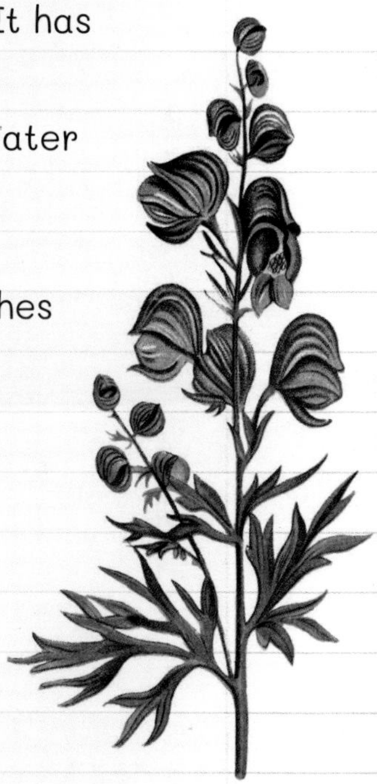

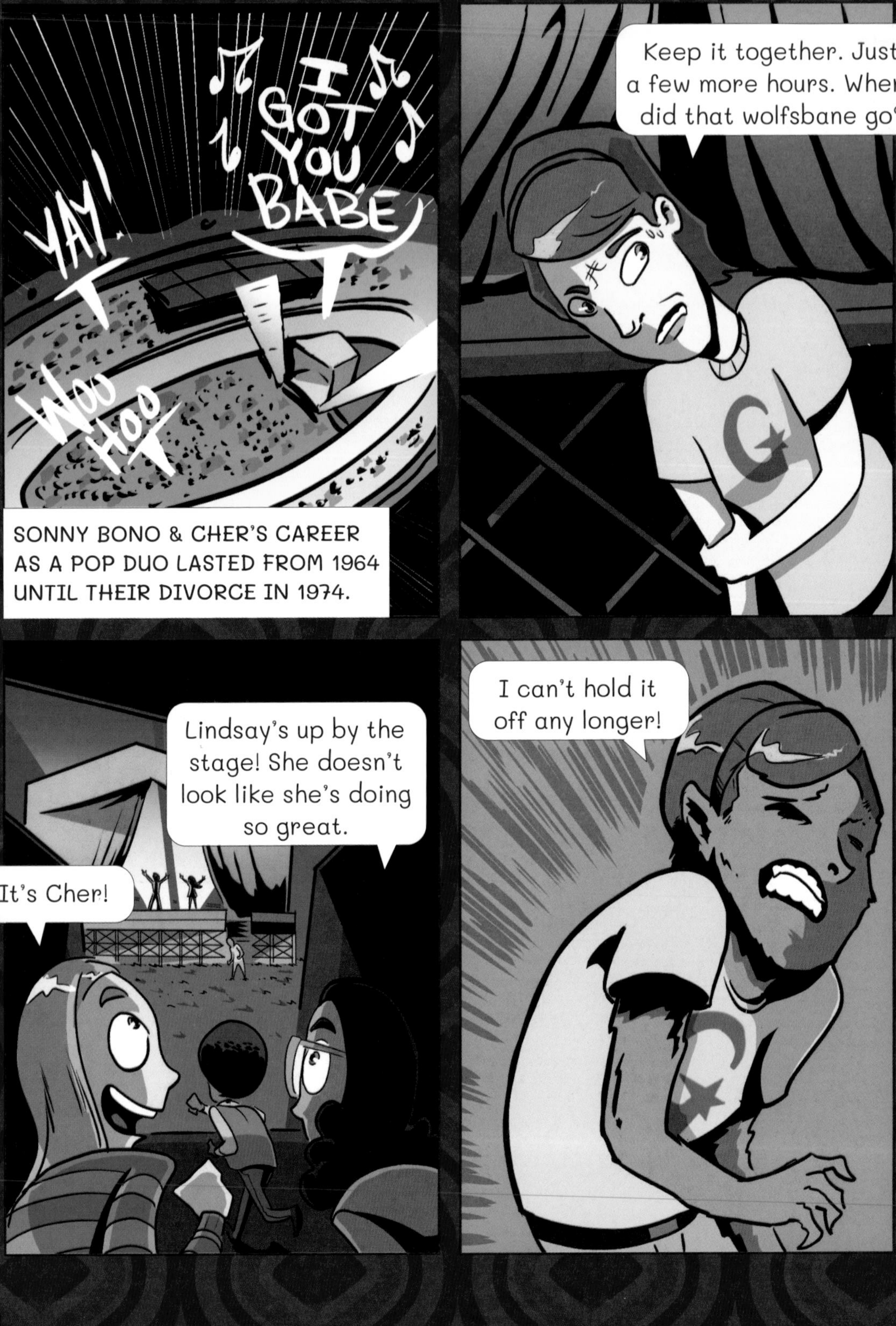
I GOT YOU BABE
YAY!
WOO HOO
SONNY BONO & CHER'S CAREER AS A POP DUO LASTED FROM 1964 UNTIL THEIR DIVORCE IN 1974.
Keep it together. Just a few more hours. Where did that wolfsbane go?
Lindsay's up by the stage! She doesn't look like she's doing so great.
It's Cher!
I can't hold it off any longer!

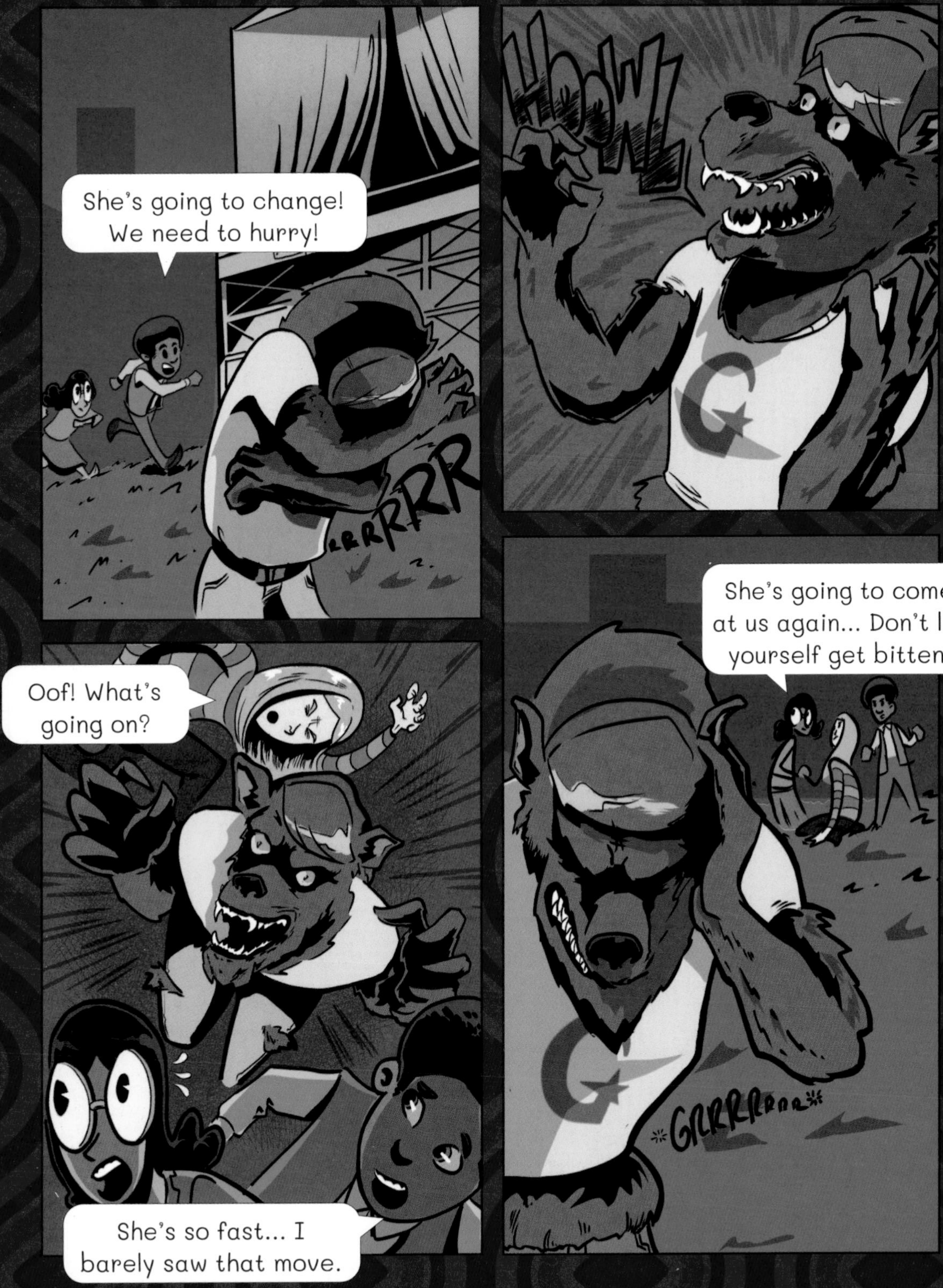

She's going to change! We need to hurry!
HOOWL
Oof! What's going on?
She's so fast... I barely saw that move.
She's going to come at us again... Don't let yourself get bitten.

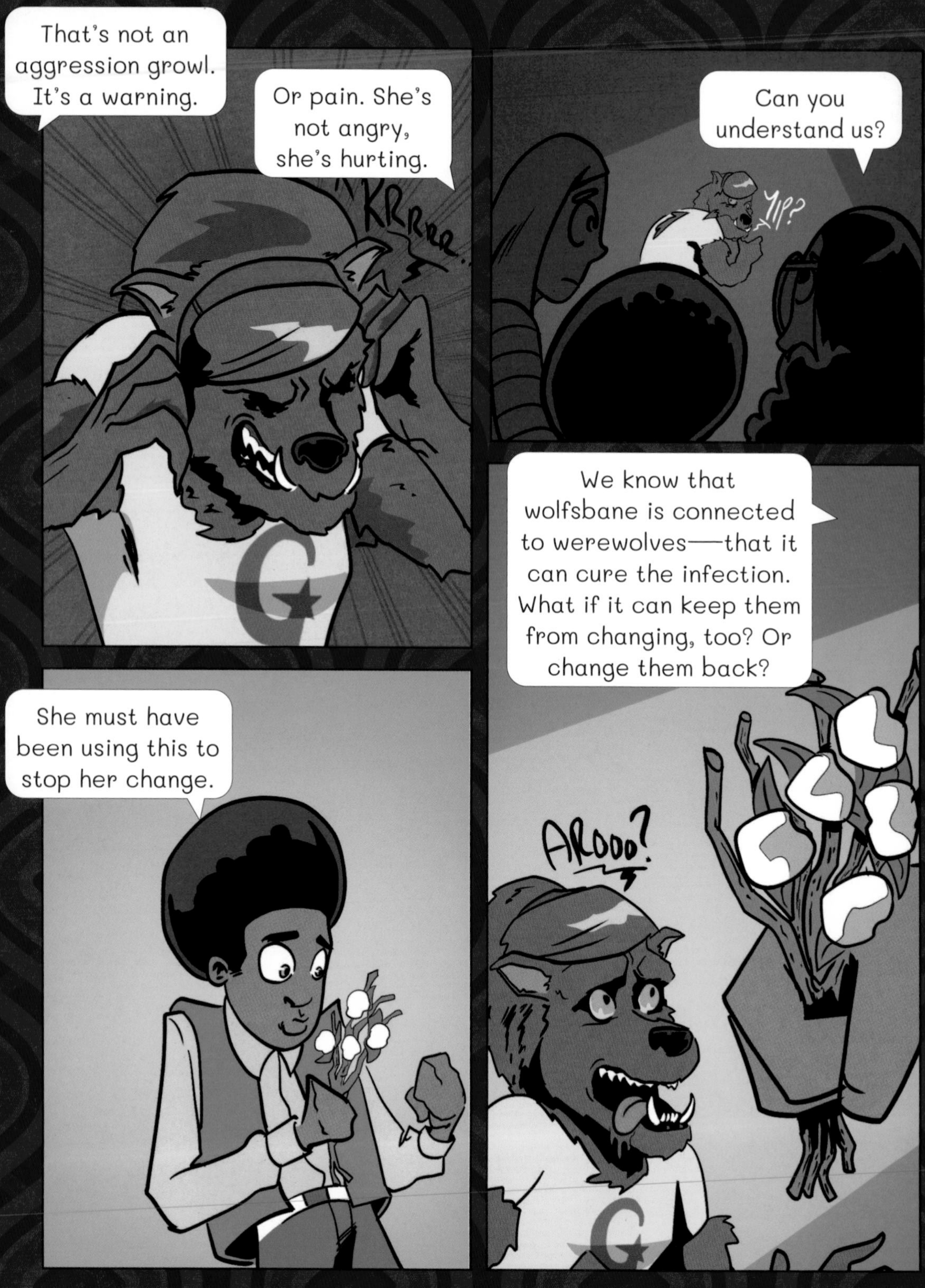
That's not an aggression growl. It's a warning.
Or pain. She's not angry, she's hurting.
KRRRR...
Can you understand us?
YIP?
We know that wolfsbane is connected to werewolves—that it can cure the infection. What if it can keep them from changing, too? Or change them back?
She must have been using this to stop her change.
AROOO?

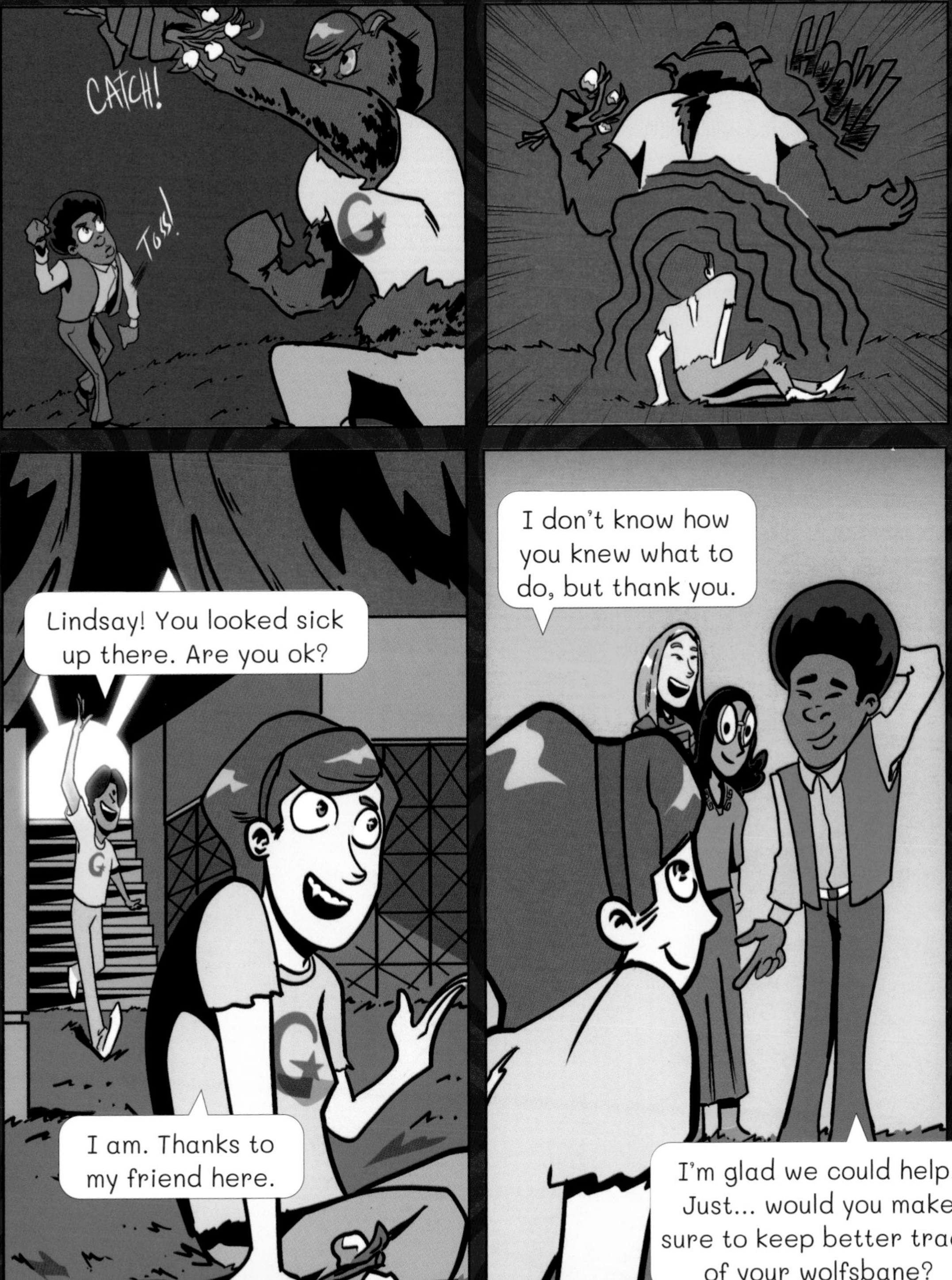
CATCH!
Toss!
Lindsay! You looked sick up there. Are you ok?
I am. Thanks to my friend here.
I don't know how you knew what to do, but thank you.
I'm glad we could help. Just... would you make sure to keep better track of your wolfsbane?

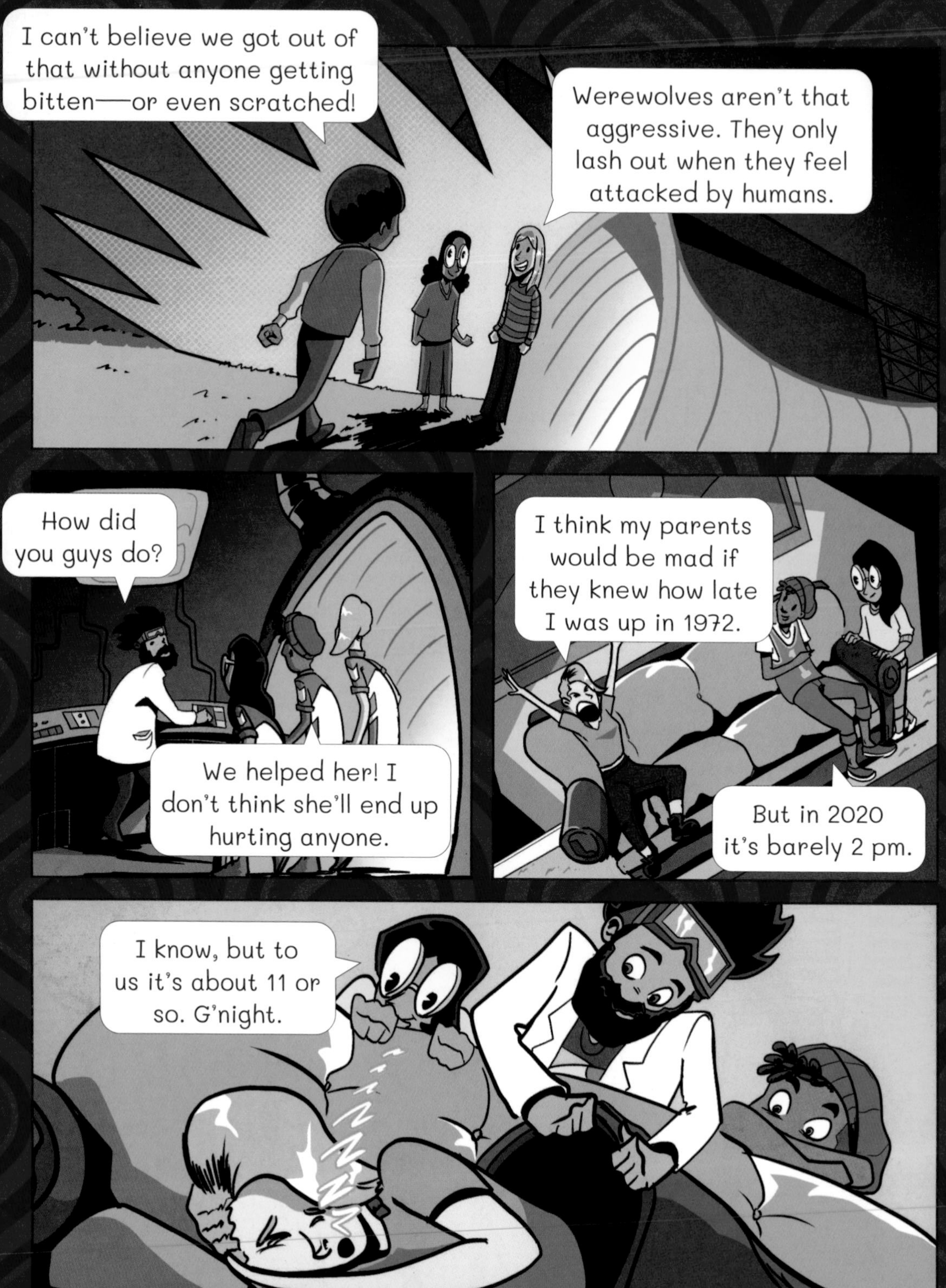
I can't believe we got out of that without anyone getting bitten—or even scratched!
Werewolves aren't that aggressive. They only lash out when they feel attacked by humans.
How did you guys do?
We helped her! I don't think she'll end up hurting anyone.
I think my parents would be mad if they knew how late I was up in 1972.
But in 2020 it's barely 2 pm.
I know, but to us it's about 11 or so. G'night.

PACKING LIST

Fashion was slightly different in the early 70s than in the later 70s.

* Bell bottom pants were popular for both men and women.
* Ponchos and frayed jeans were also in fashion.
* Patchwork and plaid became very popular.
* Men wore brightly colored suits in patterns like paisley or textures like corduroy or velvet.

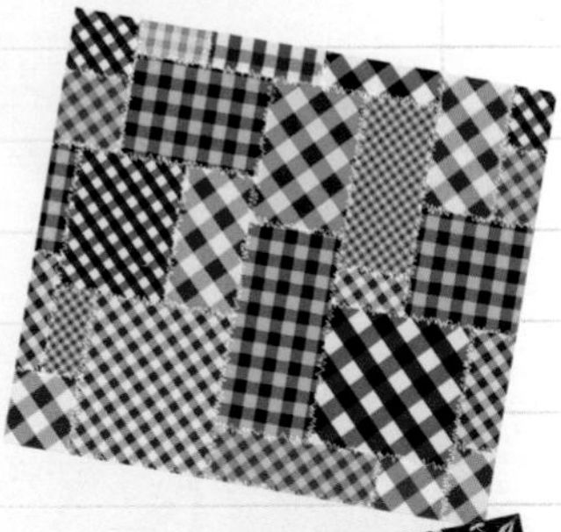

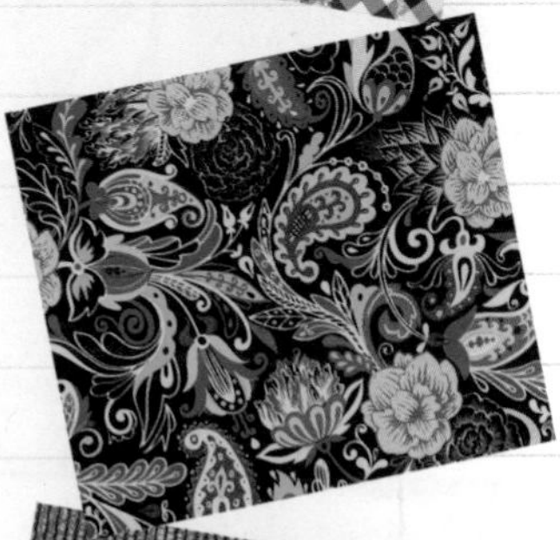

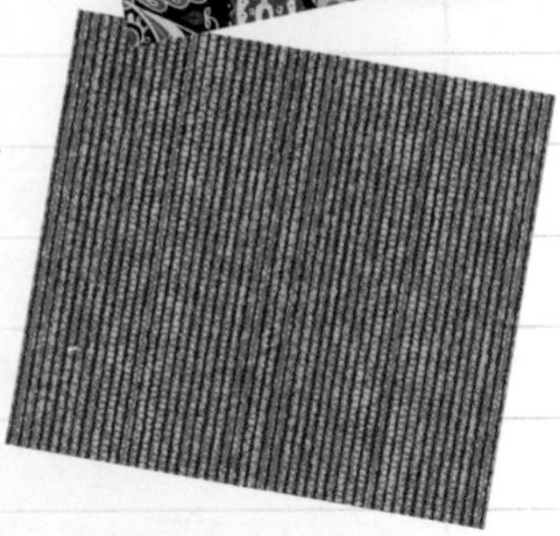

Disco style took over later in the decade. One key part of the style was the famous wrap dress from Diane von Furstenberg. It showed that women wanted comfort and function in their fashion. Men's disco style included wide **lapels** and collars.

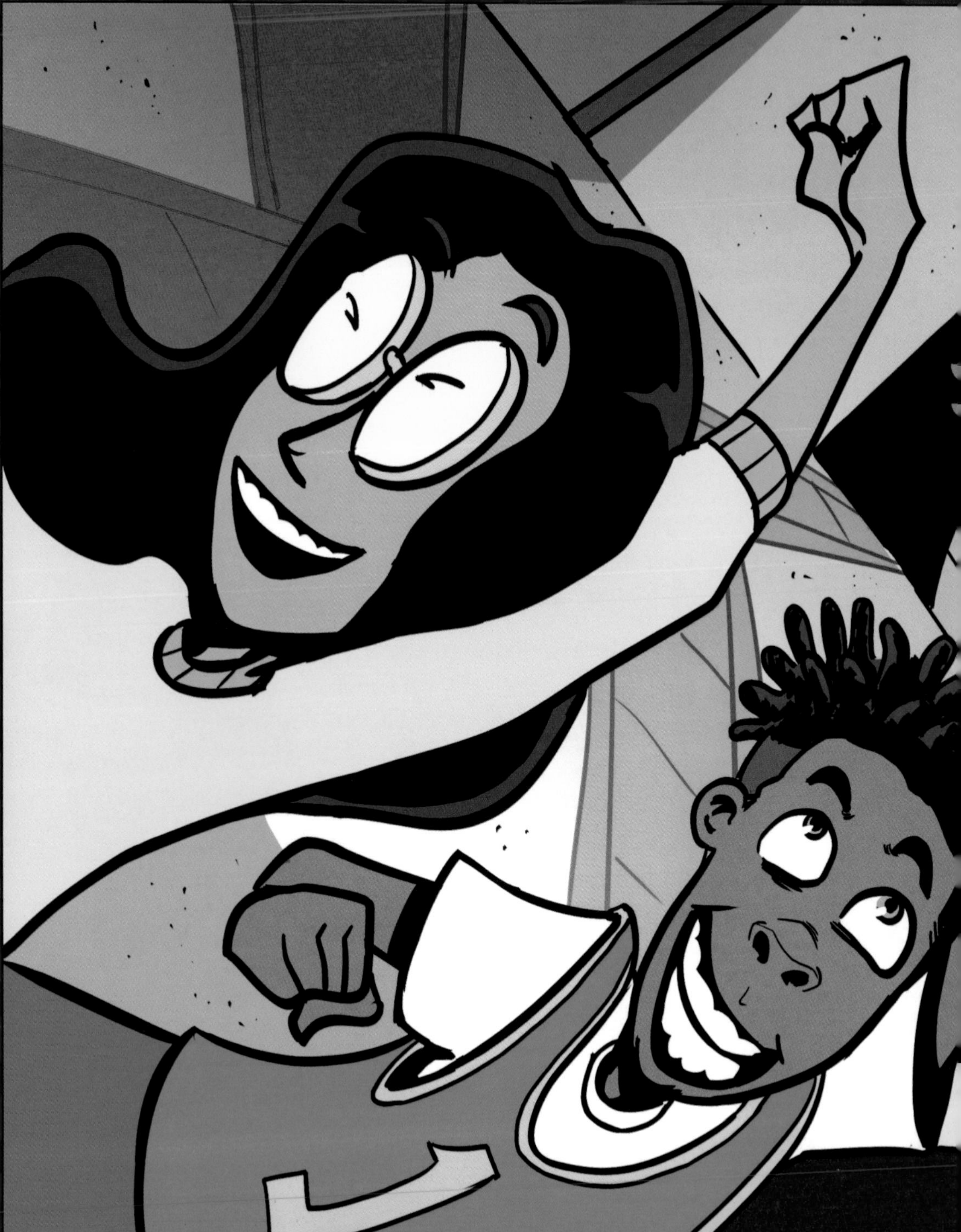

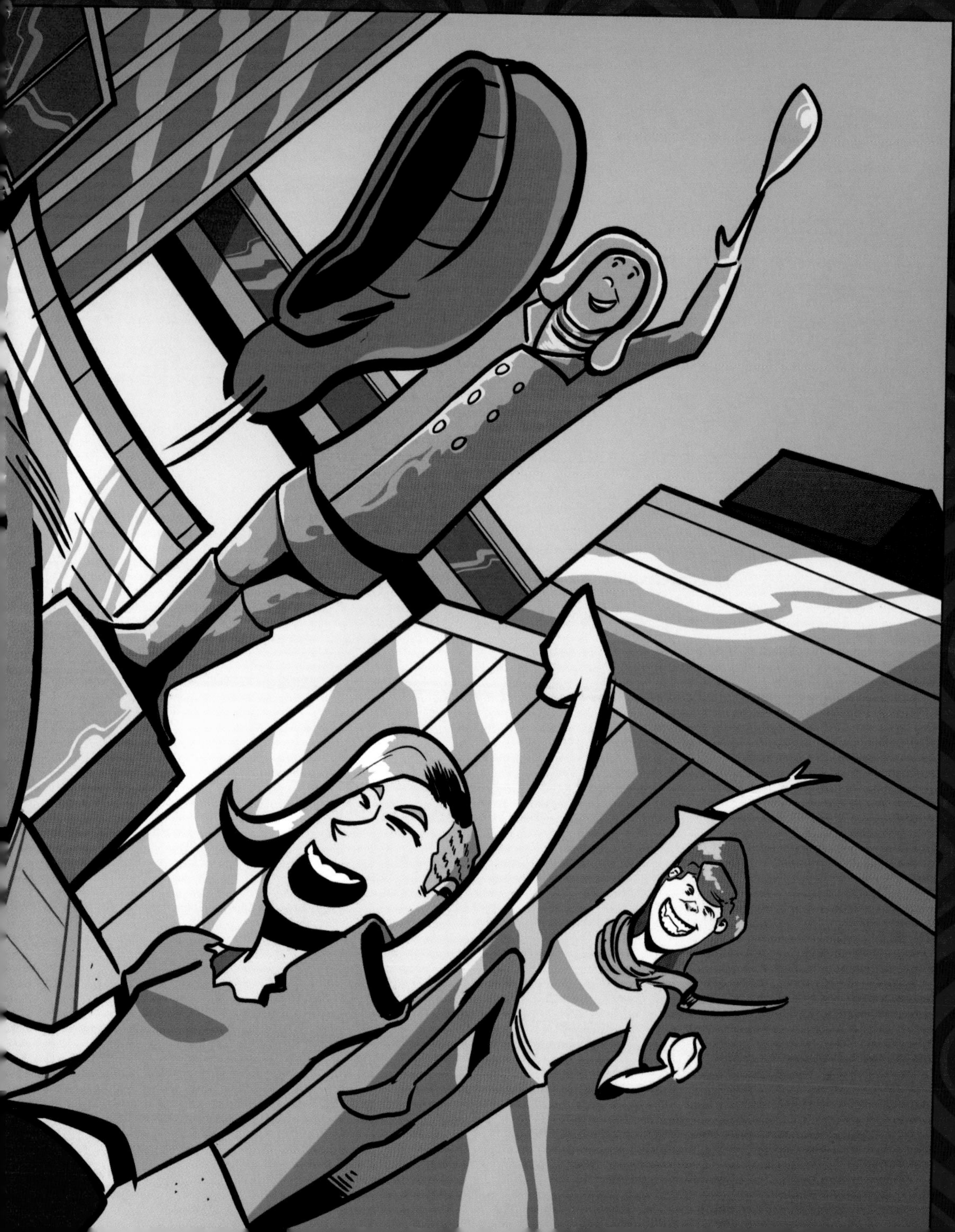

PERFORM A PLAY

Acting is an ancient art form that has only grown in popularity. Theater performances have been around since the time of the ancient Greeks.

To put on a play, you will need to collaborate with at least two to three friends. But the more the merrier!

1. Together, choose a story that you all know well. This story can come from a book, a favorite show, or a movie.

2. Next, choose parts. Which characters need to be in each scene? Who will perform as which characters?

3. Think about setting. Where does this story take place? Maybe the story takes place in a garden or park.

4. Next, decide who says what and when.

5. Using a paper and pencil, write down each character's lines. Use the paper to help you remember what each character says. Make enough copies for everyone.

With enough practice you'll be able to perform your play by memory!

LEARN MORE

BOOKS

Schwabacher, Martin. *Minnesota*. North Mankato, MN: Children's Press, 2019.

O'Connor, Jim, and Tim Foley. *What Was the Vietnam War?* New York, NY: Penguin Workshop, 2019.

WEBSITES

Ducksters—Vietnam War
https://www.ducksters.com/history/cold_war/vietnam_war.php

History—The 1970s
https://www.history.com/topics/1970s/1970s-1

National Geographic Kids—Minnesota
https://kids.nationalgeographic.com/explore/states/minnesota

THE MONSTER HUNTER TEAM

JORGE
TÍO HECTOR'S NEPHEW, JORGE, LOVES MUSIC. AT 16 HE IS ONE OF THE OLDEST MONSTER HUNTERS AND LEADER OF THE GROUP.

MARCUS
MARCUS IS 14 AND IS WISE BEYOND HIS YEARS. HE IS A PROBLEM SOLVER, OFTEN GETTING THE GROUP OUT OF STICKY SITUATIONS.

FIONA
FIONA IS FIERCE AND PROTECTIVE. AT 16 SHE IS A ROLLER DERBY CHAMPION AND IS ONE OF JORGE'S CLOSEST FRIENDS.

ELENA
ELENA IS JORGE'S LITTLE SISTER AND TÍO HECTOR'S NIECE. AT 14, SHE IS THE HEART AND SOUL OF THE GROUP. ELENA IS KIND, THOUGHTFUL, AND SINCERE.

AMY
AMY IS 15. SHE LOVES BOOKS AND HISTORY. AMY AND ELENA SPEND ALMOST EVERY WEEKEND TOGETHER. THEY ARE ATTACHED AT THE HIP.

TÍO HECTOR
JORGE AND ELENA'S TIO IS THE MASTERMIND BEHIND THE MONSTER HUNTERS. HIS TIME TRAVEL MACHINE MAKES IT ALL POSSIBLE.

GLOSSARY

Chicanos (chih-KAH-nohz) people of Mexican decscent, who live in the United States

draft (DRAFT) when the government forces people to join the military

lapels (luh-PELZ) the folds of fabric below the collar on the front of a coat or jacket

production (pro-DUHK-shun) in theater, a group in charge of the practical aspects of a play, like set design and lights; the process involved in making a play

repertory (REH-pur-tor-ee) regular performances by a theater company

sobrina (soh-BREE-nuh) "niece" in Spanish

tío (TEE-oh) "uncle" in Spanish

transformations (tranz-for-MAY-shunz) changes in form or appearance

INDEX